Jamaica's Find

Jamaica's Find

Juanita Havill

Illustrations by Anne Sibley O'Brien

Houghton Mifflin Company   Boston 1986

JP

For Laurence-Aimée
—J. H.

For my models, Brandy and Maygann
—A. S. O'B.

Library of Congress Cataloging in Publication Data

Havill, Juanita.
  Jamaica's find.

  Summary: A little girl finds a stuffed dog in the
park and decides to take it home.
  [1. Lost and found possessions—Fiction]
I. Title.
PZ7.H31115Jam   1986   [E]   85-14542
ISBN 0-395-39376-0

Text copyright © 1986 by Juanita Havill
Illustrations © 1986 by Anne Sibley O'Brien

Printed in the United States of America

Y   10 9 8 7 6 5 4 3 2 1

When Jamaica arrived at the park, there was no one there. It was almost supper time, but she still had a few minutes to play.

She sat in a swing, pushed off with her toes, and began
pumping. It was fun not to have to watch out for the little ones
who always ran in front of the swings.

Then she climbed up the slide. There was a red sock hat on the ladder step. Jamaica took it for a ride. She slid down so fast that she fell in the sand and lay flat on her back.

When she rolled over to get up, she saw a stuffed dog beside her. It was a cuddly gray dog, worn from hugging. All over it were faded food and grass stains. Its button nose must have fallen off. There was a round white spot in its place. Two black ears hung from its head.

Jamaica put the dog in her bicycle basket.

She took the hat into the park house and gave it to the young man at the counter.

The first thing her mother said when Jamaica came in the door was: "Where did that dog come from?"

"The park. I stopped to play on the way home," Jamaica said. "I found someone's red hat and took it to the Lost and Found."

"But, Jamaica, you should have returned the dog, too," said her mother. Then she said, "I'm glad you returned the hat."

"It didn't fit me," Jamaica said.

"Maybe the dog doesn't fit you either," her mother said.

"I like the dog," said Jamaica.

"Don't put that silly dog on the table!" Jamaica's brother said.

"You don't know where it came from. It isn't very clean, you know," her father said.

"Not in the kitchen, Jamaica," her mother said. Jamaica took the dog to her room. She could hear her mother say, "It probably belongs to a girl just like Jamaica."

After dessert Jamaica went to her room very quietly. She held the dog up and looked at it closely. Then she tossed it on a chair.

"Jamaica," her mother called from the kitchen. "Have you forgotten? It's your turn to dry the dishes."

"Do I have to, Mother? I don't feel good," Jamaica answered.

Jamaica heard the pots rattle. Then she heard her mother's steps.

Her mother came in quietly, sat down by Jamaica, and looked
at the stuffed dog, which lay alone on the chair. She didn't say
anything. After a while she put her arms around Jamaica and
squeezed for a long time.

"Mother, I want to take the dog back to the park," Jamaica said.

"We'll go first thing in the morning." Her mother smiled.

Jamaica ran to the park house and plopped the stuffed dog on the counter.

"I found this by the slide," she told the young man.

"Oh, hi. Aren't you the girl who gave me the hat last night?"

"Yes," said Jamaica, feeling hot around her ears.

"You sure do find a lot of things. I'll put it on the Lost and Found shelf."

Jamaica stood watching him.

"Is that all?" he asked. "You didn't find anything else, did you?"

"No. That's all." She stayed to watch him put the dog on a shelf behind him.

"I'm sure some little girl or boy will come in after it today, a nice little dog like that," the young man said.

Jamaica ran outside. She didn't feel like playing alone. There
was no one else at the park but her mother, who sat on a bench.
Then Jamaica saw a girl and her mother cross the street to the park.
"Hi. I'm Jamaica. What's your name?" she said to the girl.

The girl let go of her mother's hand. "Kristin," she said.
"Do you want to climb the jungle gym with me, Kristin?"
Jamaica said.

Kristin ran toward Jamaica. "Yes, but I have to find something first."

"What?" asked Jamaica. Kristin was bending under the slide.

"What did you lose?" said Jamaica.

"Edgar dog. I brought him with me yesterday and now I can't find him," Kristin answered.

"Was he kind of gray with black ears?" Jamaica couldn't keep from shouting. "Come along with me."

The young man in the park house looked over the counter at the two girls.

"Now what have you found?" he asked Jamaica.

But this time Jamaica didn't drop anything onto the counter. Instead, she smiled her biggest smile. "I found the girl who belongs to that stuffed dog."

Jamaica was almost as happy as Kristin, who took Edgar dog in her arms and gave him a big welcome-back hug.